WHAT'S THE DIFFERENCE?

AN ENDANGERED ANIMAL SUBTRACTION STORY

BY SUZANNE SLADE
ILLUSTRATED BY JOAN WAITES

Our world is filled with fascinating animals. Sadly, some of these beautiful animals are endangered, or in danger of disappearing forever. Through the years, animals have been harmed by pollution, loss of habitat, and over-hunting.

Fortunately, many people are working hard to save these animals and are making a big difference in our world. They restore and protect natural habitats, teach people how to take care of the environment, and raise certain animals in captivity. Their hard work has increased the populations of many endangered animals. By working together, people have made a huge difference!

In the 1960s many bald eagle eggs began breaking before the eaglets hatched. Scientists discovered the mothers ate fish from lakes polluted with DDT, a chemical farmers used to kill insects. The DDT was making the egg shells too thin and was banned in 1972. One of the first animals protected under the Endangered Species Act of 1973, the bald eagle's population has grown from fewer than 1000 in the 1960s to over 20,000 today. They are now recovered, or no longer endangered!

3 - 2 = ?

Three sleeping eaglets wake;
each looks like the rest.
Two stretch their wings and fly.
How many in the nest?

Utah prairie dogs were declared endangered in 1973 due to poisoning, trapping, shooting, and habitat loss. People created safe places for these animals to live and now move them to safe places before habitats are destroyed. Their numbers have improved, and today this playful mammal is listed as threatened, the stage before endangered.

6 - 1 = ?

Six silly prairie dogs
frolic most the day.
One guards the colony.
How many dogs at play?

8 - 3 = ?

Beautiful Karner blue butterflies live in sandy dunes, pine barrens, oak savannahs, and prairies where wild lupine plants grow. These habitats are now rare, and Karner blues have been endangered since 1992. People have been helping these beautiful insects by restoring their habitat. Some school children grow wild lupine to feed the caterpillars, and a few zoos raise the butterflies to set free in the wild.

Eight graceful butterflies
soaring way up high—
three stop to rest their wings.
How many in the sky?

Known for their loud "whooping" cries, whooping cranes are the tallest birds in North America (5 ft. or 1.5m)! When their wetland homes were drained and turned into farms, many died. Now that they are protected as endangered animals, some are raised by people and taught migration routes by following small planes!

10 - 5 = ?

Ten dancing whooping cranes
lose their wetland home.
Five find a refuge near.
How many cranes still roam?

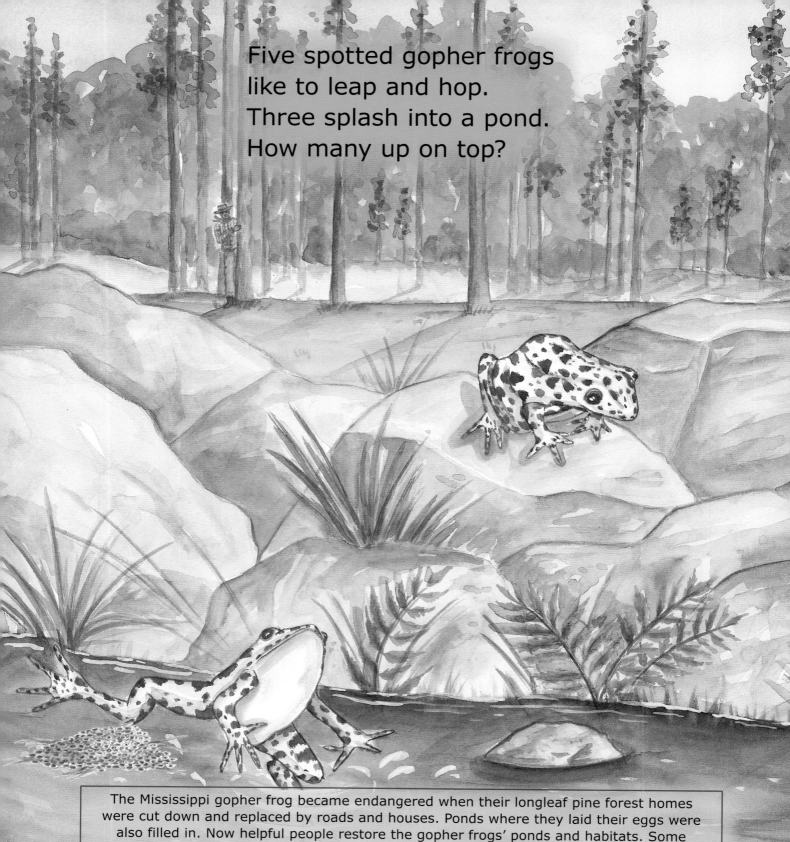

Five spotted gopher frogs
like to leap and hop.
Three splash into a pond.
How many up on top?

The Mississippi gopher frog became endangered when their longleaf pine forest homes were cut down and replaced by roads and houses. Ponds where they laid their eggs were also filled in. Now helpful people restore the gopher frogs' ponds and habitats. Some of these precious frogs also live in zoos to keep them safe. All this hard work will mean more of these leaping amphibians in the future!

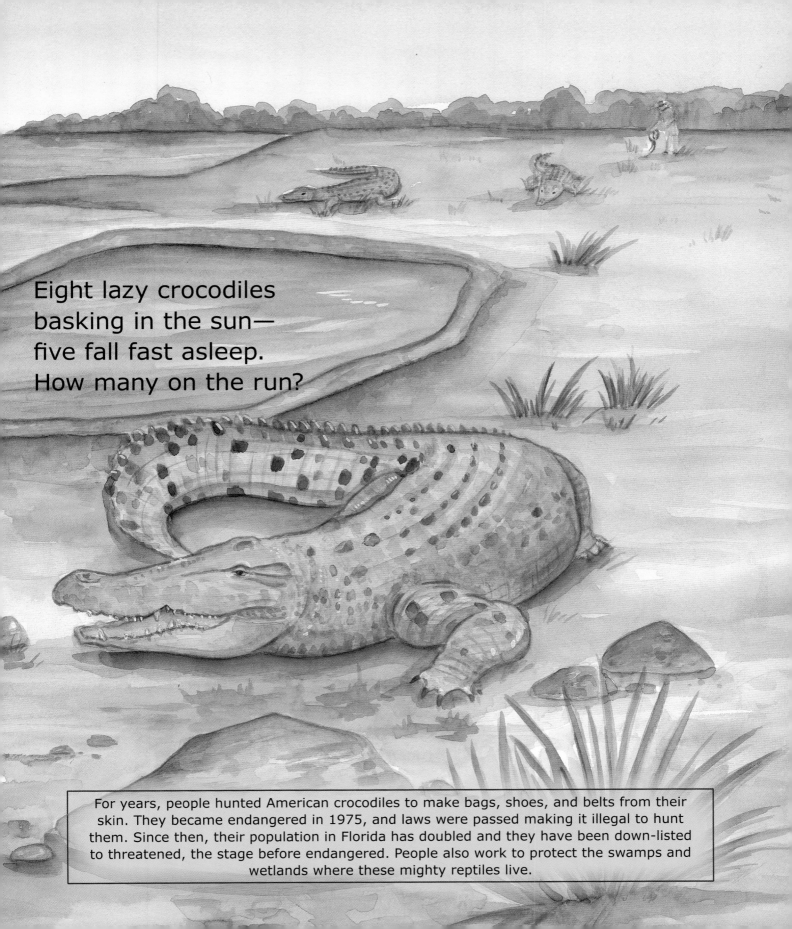

Eight lazy crocodiles
basking in the sun—
five fall fast asleep.
How many on the run?

For years, people hunted American crocodiles to make bags, shoes, and belts from their skin. They became endangered in 1975, and laws were passed making it illegal to hunt them. Since then, their population in Florida has doubled and they have been down-listed to threatened, the stage before endangered. People also work to protect the swamps and wetlands where these mighty reptiles live.

Atlantic salmon lay small, orange eggs on rock nests in rivers. Tiny fish hatch from these eggs and grow for about two years until they are 5 to 6 inches (12 to 15 cm) long. At this stage, they are called smolts. Smolts swim down rivers to the salty sea where they grow into adults. Atlantic salmon are endangered because of over-fishing, pollution, dam building, and habitat loss. New fishing laws, fishing vessels limiting their catch, dam removal, fish ladders, and man-made channels are helping the salmon population grow.

Six splashing salmon smolts
heading out to sea—
four find an ocean school.
How many swimming free?

6 - 4 = ?

Bowhead whales became endangered in 1970 because of commercial over-hunting. Found only in the Arctic, these giant marine mammals migrate south to the warmer waters of the sub-Arctic for winter. The International Whaling Commission (IWC) now watches over the hunting of these important animals.

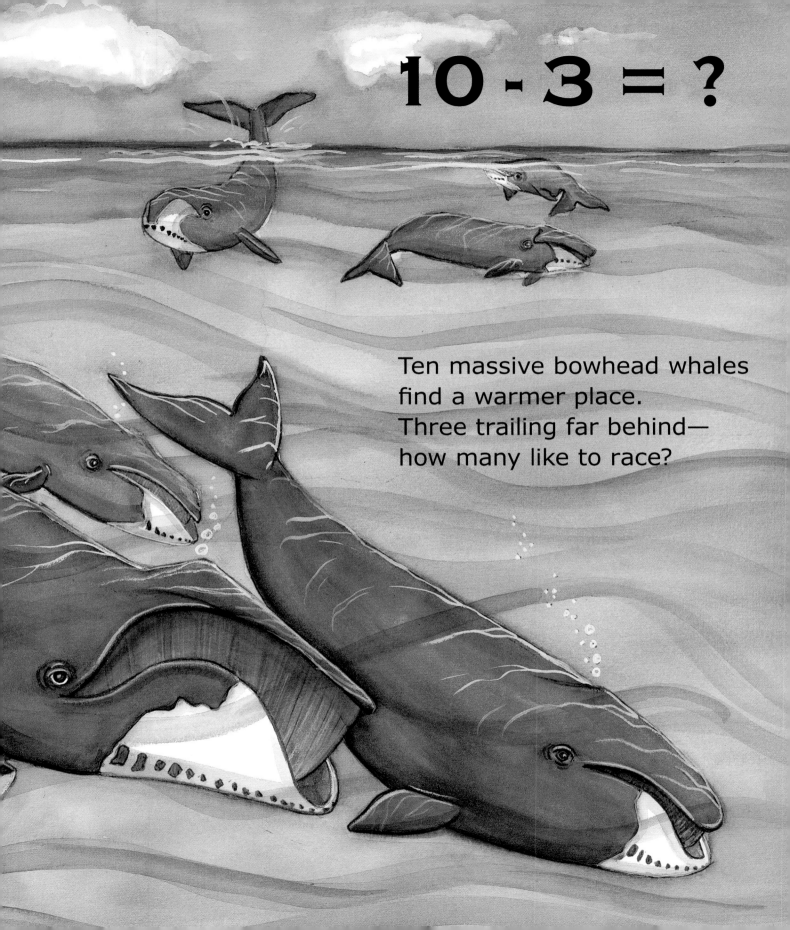

10 - 3 = ?

Ten massive bowhead whales
find a warmer place.
Three trailing far behind—
how many like to race?

Nine munching manatees
grazing in the bay—
three drift in close to shore.
How many far away?

9 - 3 = ?

Long ago, people hunted West Indian (Florida) manatees to make lamp oil and leather. Today, these slow-moving, endangered animals are still in danger due to loss of warm water habitats and fast-moving boats that accidentally hit them. Now there are special areas where boats are not allowed to go or must go slowly. People are also restoring warm-water habitats and this marine mammal's population is rising!

SLOW

Twelve furry otter pups
in a grassy bed—
two hunt for clams below.
How many rest instead?

The smallest of marine mammals, Southern sea otters dive to the ocean floor to gather clams, abalone, and sea urchins. They bring their tasty treats to the surface to dine while floating on their backs. Long ago, fur traders killed so many sea otters that they were almost extinct. Today, the Marine Mammal Protection Act of 1972 and the Endangered Species Act of 1973 protect otters from fur-hunters. People also protect them from fishing nets and crab traps.

12 - 2 = ?

Gray bats hibernate inside warm caves during winter. If wakened by noisy visitors, they become frightened and fly away. Most will never come back. There are only about nine caves in the U.S. where endangered gray bats can hibernate, and the openings of some have been blocked. Since 1970 the number of these flying mammals has dropped in half. People are now working hard to protect their caves.

Nine silent snoozing bats
snuggle in a cave.
Six frightened by some noise—
how many bats are brave?

9 - 6 = ?

5 - 2 = ?

Five lonely red wolves howl
under bright moonlight.
Two run inside their den.
How many walk the night?

Once common in the Southeastern United States, red wolves were hunted to near extinction. They were listed as an endangered species in 1967, and biologists captured the few remaining animals in the wild. The wolves were put in captivity to keep them safe and to breed more pups. In 1987, a few adults were released in North Carolina, and the family packs grew. Now there are over 100 in the wild!

Every day conservationists, biologists, zoo workers, and children work hard to help animals in danger. They are making a big difference in endangered animal populations around the world. Now that's something to celebrate!

Kind, caring people
work from dawn till late
helping lots of creatures.
Let's all go celebrate!

For Creative Minds

Endangered Animal Vocabulary

Extinct: A species that is no longer alive anywhere on earth—extinction is forever.

Recovered: A species that has been removed (delisted) from the Federal Endangered Species Act's list.

Endangered: A species in a lot of trouble—it may become extinct if people don't help out.

Downlisted: A species' recovery showing enough improvement to have listing changed (e.g. endangered to threatened).

Threatened: A species in trouble—it may become endangered if people don't help out.

Habitat: Where the animals live and can find everything they need to survive: food, water, shelter, and a safe place to raise their families.

Food Chains & Webs

Our earth is filled with millions of different animals. All animals need energy to live and grow. They get this energy from the food they eat. Animals depend on one another, and are connected to each other, by food chains. A food web is made of many food chains which have some of the same animals or plants.

Food chains begin with plants. Plants are known as producers because they make their own food using energy from the sun in a process called photosynthesis.

Animals that eat plants are called herbivores. When animals munch on tasty plants, they get some of the sun's energy which is stored inside plants.

People are at the top of many food chains. Can you think of other animals that are at the top of their food chains?

Carnivores are animals that eat meat or other animals. Carnivores also get energy from the sun because they eat animals that have eaten plants.

Animals that eat both plants and animals are called omnivores. Living things that eat other living things are called consumers. Herbivores, carnivores, and omnivores are all consumers.

Missing Links in Food Chains

Animals and plants in a habitat are connected to each other in food chains and webs. If the population of one animal decreases, or if an endangered animal becomes extinct, this loss affects many other animals in its food chains and webs.

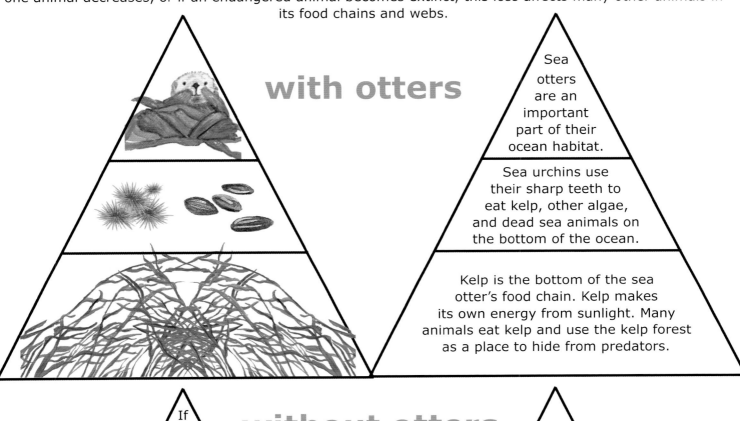

with otters

Sea otters are an important part of their ocean habitat.

Sea urchins use their sharp teeth to eat kelp, other algae, and dead sea animals on the bottom of the ocean.

Kelp is the bottom of the sea otter's food chain. Kelp makes its own energy from sunlight. Many animals eat kelp and use the kelp forest as a place to hide from predators.

without otters (called "urchin barren")

If sea otters disappear, the urchins would grow out of control.

Too many urchins would devour the kelp forest, leaving no food for other plant-eaters such as small fish and crabs.

And, with no safe place to hide, young fish are easy prey and begin to disappear too. Without sea otters, a busy ocean habitat will soon have few animals and plants left.

Endangered Animals

Use the information found in the book to answer the questions below. Answers are upside down at the bottom of this page.

gray bat

Myotis grisescens

red wolf

Canis rufus

Utah prairie dog

Cynomys parvidens

Karner blue butterfy

Lycaeides melissa

whooping crane

Grus americana

Mississippi gopher frog

Rana capito sevosa

bald eagle

Haliaeetus leucocephalus

Atlantic salmon

Salmo salar

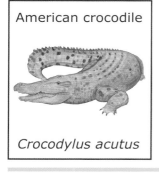

American crocodile

Crocodylus acutus

Southern sea otter

Enhydra lutris nereis

West Indian manatees

Trichechus manatus

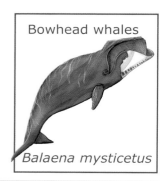

Bowhead whales

Balaena mysticetus

1. Which animals are mammals, reptiles, fish, birds, insects, or amphibians?
2. Which animals are currently federally listed as endangered, threatened, or recovered?
3. Which animals are marine mammals (mammals that live in the ocean)?

Fact Families

Just as animals in a family are related to each other, numbers in a fact family are related too. The three numbers in each fact family below are related to each other by the four math facts beside them.

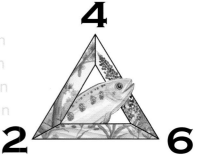

4

2   **6**

4 salmon + **?** salmon = **6** salmon

2 salmon + **4** salmon = **?** salmon

6 salmon - **4** salmon = **?** salmon

? salmon - **2** salmon = **4** salmon

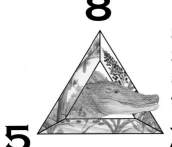

8

5   **3**

5 crocodiles + **?** crocodiles = **8** crocodiles

3 crocodiles + **5** crocodiles = **?** crocodiles

8 crocodiles - **5** crocodiles = **?** crocodiles

? crocodiles - **3** crocodiles = **5** crocodiles

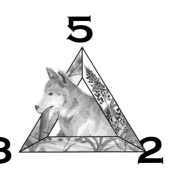

5

3   **2**

? wolves + **2** wolves = **5** wolves

2 wolves + **3** wolves = **?** wolves

5 wolves - **2** wolves = **?** wolves

? wolves - **3** wolves = **2** wolves

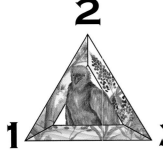

2

1   **3**

2 eaglets + **?** eaglets = **3** eaglets

1 eaglet + **2** eaglets = **?** eaglets

3 eaglets - **2** eaglets = **?** eaglets

? eaglets - **1** eaglet   = **2** eaglets

8

3   **5**

3 butterflies + **?** butterflies = **8** butterflies

5 butterflies + **3** butterflies = **?** butterflies

8 butterflies - **5** butterflies = **?** butterflies

? butterflies - **5** butterflies = **3** butterflies

To my children, Christina and Patrick, who have made a wonderful difference in my life!
And a special thanks to Tom Stehn, Whooping Crane Coordinator, US Fish and Wildlife Service,
and Dawn Jennings, US Fish and Wildlife Service, Jacksonville Ecological Services Office, for
their research assistance. — SS

For my three finest works of art: Taylor, Caitrin and Haley — JW

Thanks to Kelly Ann Bibb, Recovery Coordinator, Endangered Species Program, US Fish and
Wildlife Service Southeast Region and Terri Jacobson, Wildlife Biologist & Environmental
Education Specialist, Endangered Species Field Office, US Fish and Wildlife Service for
verifying the accuracy of the information in this book.

Publisher's Cataloging-In-Publication Data
Slade, Suzanne.
What's the difference? : an endangered animal subtraction story / by Suzanne Slade ;
illustrated by Joan Waites.

p. : chiefly col. ill. ; cm.

Summary: Threatened and endangered animals are found all over the world, in all
different types of habitats. Readers celebrate the huge difference that caring people make
for these animals while practicing subtraction skills. Each animal is presented through a
clever rhyming verse and subtraction problem. Includes "For Creative Minds" section.

ISBN: 9781607180708 (hardcover)
ISBN: 9781607180814 (pbk.)
Also available in auto-flip, auto-read, 3D-page-curling, and selectable English and
Spanish text and audio eBooks
Interest level: 004-008.
Grade level: P-3.
Lexile Level: 960 Lexile Code: AD

1. Endangered species--Juvenile literature. 2. Subtraction--Juvenile literature. 3.
Endangered species. 4. Subtraction. I. Waites, Joan C.
II. Title.

QL83 .S52 2010
591.68   2009937787

Manufactured in China, January, 2010
This product conforms to CPSIA 2008
First Printing

Sylvan Dell Publishing
976 Houston Northcutt Blvd., Suite 3
Mt. Pleasant, SC 29464